Tim Mouse
Goes Down the Stream

For Paul

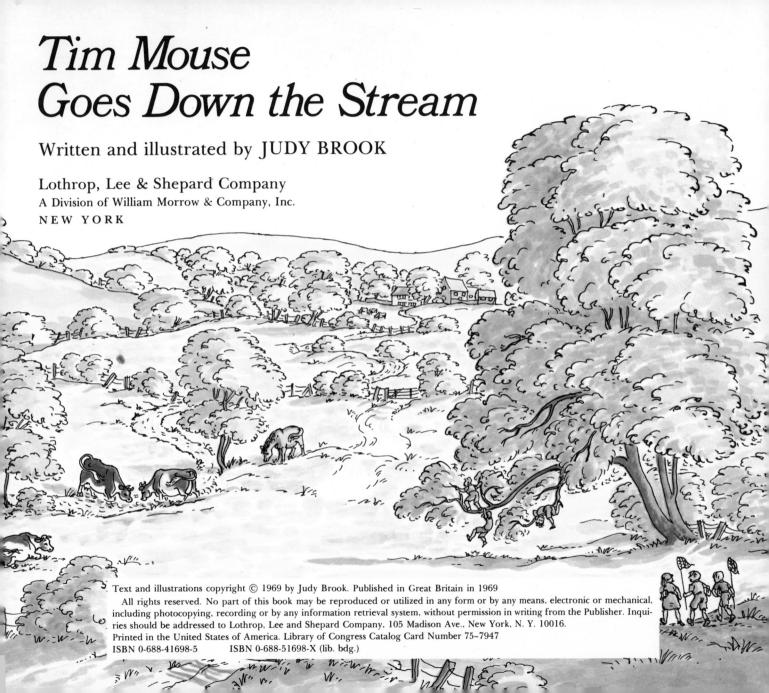

Tim Mouse
Goes Down the Stream

Written and illustrated by JUDY BROOK

Lothrop, Lee & Shepard Company
A Division of William Morrow & Company, Inc.
NEW YORK

2134658

One warm sunny afternoon, Tim Mouse and
Mr. Brown were sailing paper boats on the
stream when a bottle floated past.
"Maybe there is a message inside," said Tim,
and he fished the bottle out of the water.

There certainly was a message! It said:

"HELP! I've been captured by a gang of fierce river rats. PLEASE PLEASE come to my rescue. Willy Frog."

"Oh, how terrible," said Tim. "But where is the rats' hideout? Quick, we must go up the stream to find them, and rescue poor Willy Frog."

They raced along the banks of the stream until they came to Tim's little raft, beautifully made out of sticks and string with a small mast and sail.

Tim unfurled the sail, helped Mr. Brown on board, and pushed off from the bank.

Mr. Brown had never been on any kind of boat before. He sat nervously on the seat, clutching the mast.

First they went to Willy Frog's house. They could not find him or any clues to where the rats had taken him. Just when they were

wondering which way to go, a little minnow called from the water:
"I know where Willy Frog is—fierce river rats have caught him.
Quick, quick! Come with me and I'll lead you to their hideout."

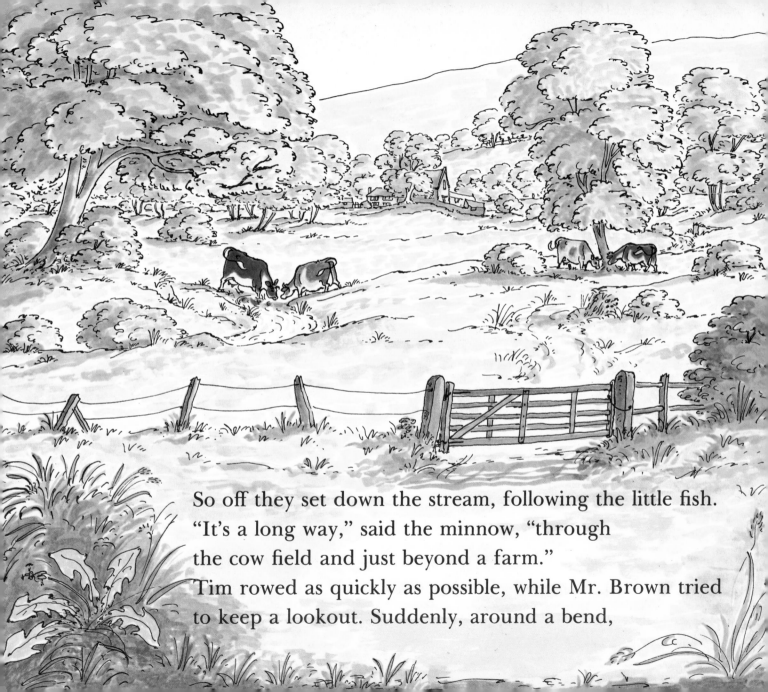

So off they set down the stream, following the little fish.
"It's a long way," said the minnow, "through
the cow field and just beyond a farm."
Tim rowed as quickly as possible, while Mr. Brown tried
to keep a lookout. Suddenly, around a bend,

there were two huge cows standing in the water having a drink!
Tim pulled on the oar to try and stop, but the current took the little
raft on and on, until they were right under the two cows' enormous
wet noses!

"Moooo—what's *this*?" mooed the cows, right in Tim's and Mr. Brown's ears.

"Oooooooo, HELP—I'm being eaten!" wailed Mr. Brown at the top of his squeaky voice. And at this, the cows turned around and ran!

"Moooo," they bellowed, and lumbered out of the stream as quickly as possible, splashing mud and water everywhere and almost upsetting the little raft.

"Oooooooh, help help help, we're going to drown!" wailed Mr.
Brown, as Tim struggled to keep the raft upright.

But soon the waves subsided, and on they went again, following the little fish. Sometimes the banks of the stream were very high, with

trees growing overhead, and in places the watercress grew like a jungle. Then at last they reached the farm.

"Well well, look at that," clucked some hens. "A floating mouse and hedgehog— what is the world coming to?" "We are going to rescue Mr. Frog," said Tim. "Tut tut tut," clucked the hens, as the stream took the raft straight into—

a duck pond!
The little fish quickly hid under the raft.
"Well . . . what's this?" quacked the ducks.
"Just look underneath, there's a fish to eat!"

They dived and splashed all around Tim and Mr. Brown, trying to catch the little minnow.

"Oh quick quick, please go under the bridge," spluttered the little fish from under the raft, and Tim rowed as fast as he could.

"Get out of our way, you big bullies," shouted Mr. Brown. "We are going to rescue Mr. Frog."

"Ah-*ha*," quacked the ducks greedily.

Luckily it wasn't very far to the bridge, and soon they were safely under it, away from the ducks.

"Come quickly," called the little fish. "We are nearly there."

And sure enough, as they came out from under the bridge

there was a funny old toy boat, with a large rat
snoring away loudly on deck!

"Willy Frog is locked in one of the cabins,"
whispered the fish. "The rats are asleep now,
but they wake up at sunset. Oh hurry, hurry do!"

Tim rowed right up to the boat
and went all around it, peeping
through the portholes.
At first he could only see
the rats, asleep in their bunks
and hammocks. But then, at last,
there was poor Willy Frog
looking very miserable,

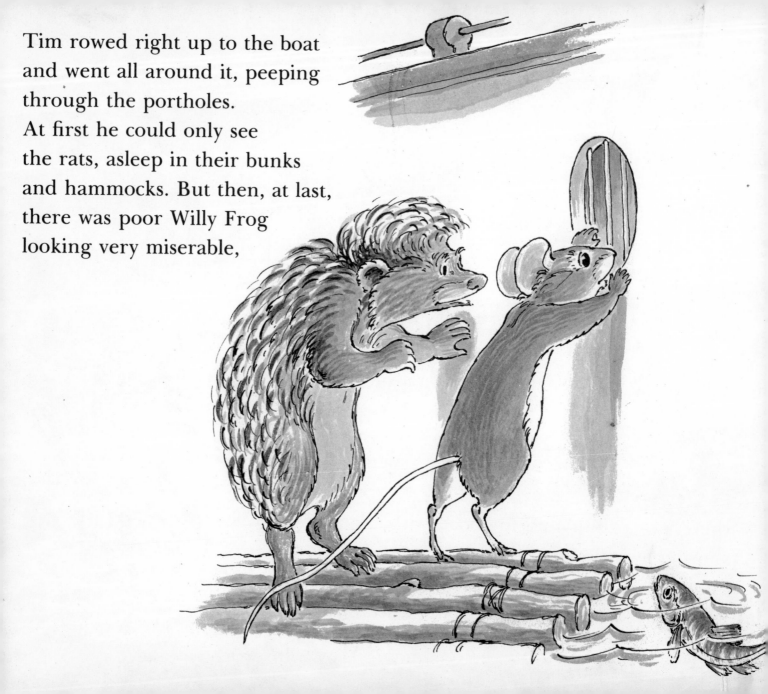

locked up in a little prison at the stern of the boat.

"Oh dear," said Tim. "I'll have to go past all the sleeping rats to rescue him. And I had better hurry—they will soon be awake!"

So Tim bravely climbed up the mooring rope
and onto the deck.

"Oh be careful, be careful," whispered Mr. Brown from below.

Trembling with fear, Tim crept toward the horrible fat guard rat, and stealthily tiptoed past him, down the steps and right into the rats' den!

Oh, how smelly and dirty it was! Tim had to creep very carefully so as not to stumble over all the rubbish on the floor and wake the four terrible snoring rats.

Then Tim gently undid the bolts on Willy Frog's prison, and quietly opened the door. "Hurry, hurry," whispered Tim. "The rats might wake up at any moment."

Willy Frog wanted to jump for joy when he saw Tim. Quietly he
followed him out of the prison and into the main cabin.
Suddenly one of the rats gave an enormous snort and scratched its
head. Tim and Willy stood frozen with fright—but, thank goodness,
the rat just turned over and went on sleeping.

They crept up the steps past the fat snoring guard rat, and
gently slipped over the sides and onto the raft, free at last.

Then Tim quietly gnawed through the mooring rope, gave the boat
a gentle push, and very slowly it began to drift away. . . .

From the rushes they watched as the toy boat, with all the rats
still snoring loudly, drifted away down the stream.
"What a shock they'll get when they wake up miles from home,"
said Willy. "Let's follow them a little way."
They paddled along behind the boat. But around the first bend,

the stream went straight through the middle of a village!
Tim quickly turned the raft around for home,

while the little boat, and the
snoring rats, drifted slowly
past some astonished children
through the village, far away
and out to sea.

Then, after Willy Frog helped Tim to row home,
what a welcome they got! Everyone came to greet
them as they heard how Tim Mouse had rescued
Willy Frog and sent the terrible rats away.
But Mr. Brown missed all the welcome. The excitement
of the day had exhausted him, and he fell fast asleep.

When they arrived at Willy Frog's house, two little harvest mice cooked them a wonderful dinner of bluebottle flies for Wi̵̵̵̵ and nut cakes for Tim and Mr. Brown.

Afterward, they sat outside by the edge of the stream, while Willy
Frog told them the long story of how he had been captured by the
horrible gang of fierce river rats.
"I wonder where they are now?" said Tim Mouse.